Horror of Montauk Cave

Karen Liberatore

A **PERSPECTIVES** BOOK
High Noon Books
Novato, California

Series Editor: Penn Mullin
Cover and Illustrations: Herb Heidinger

International Standard Book Number: 0-87879-294-5

9 8 7 6 5 4 3 2 1 0
20 19 18 17 16 15 14 13 12 11

Contents

CHAPTER 1

Return to Mokane Valley

Now and then Peter could hear an animal somewhere out there in the trees. But not another sound! He was all alone—driving in silence through the hills of Mokane Valley. Up and down, up and down the hills went, mile after mile, thick with trees. Even his car radio wouldn't work. No radio stations could be heard this far from the city. It was dark outside. He put his headlights on bright. He had been driving for hours and hours, trying to reach Centerville. Centerville, the town where he was born and grew up. Where he lived before he left to go to college. Only thirty more miles to drive, and he'd be there.

In that terrible silence he thought he could sometimes hear the Mokane River. He knew he could never forget the sounds it made. The river ran fast. It passed right by Centerville. And

Centerville was right in the middle of Mokane Valley. The sounds of the river could be heard all through Mokane Valley. Peter remembered that he used to hear them even when he was little. There were caves in the Mokane Valley that went for miles. The one he knew best was Montauk Cave. Peter used to go into it when he was a boy. Sometimes it seemed as if he were walking right under the river because the sound of the water was so close.

Now he was coming back to the Valley and to Centerville. And to Mother Jerome. That name made him turn ice cold. No one knew where she had come from. No one knew how old she was. It seemed that she had been in the Mokane Valley ever since he could remember. And she was old even then. He didn't want to, but he had to go to see her on this trip back home.

When he thought of the caves, he thought of Mother Jerome. When he thought of Mother Jerome, he thought of the caves. Peter thought the caves were the only unusual thing about Mokane Valley. He probably knew more about caves than anyone else. He even wrote books about caves. He liked to tell people about them. But not Mother Jerome. She gave him the creeps even now.

Peter had a new book to write. He was looking forward to it. There were many stories, legends, and superstitions about the caves in Mokane Valley. The largest of all the caves, Montauk, had the most legends. Peter had heard many of the stories when he was growing up. There were legends that people who went into the Montauk Cave turned into cats. And that cats were turned into people. Peter didn't believe these stories. But now it was his job to write about them. They were so strange. Why did people make them up long, long ago? Or could they be true? True or not, the people in the Mokane Valley really believed all those stories about the caves.

The good thing about going back to Centerville was that he would be able to see his sister, Anne, and her family. It had been a long time since they had all been together. It would be great to see Anne and Tom and the kids again. Let's see, he thought. Jasper must be about 17 now and Owen about 15. And Susie—maybe about 13.

Again Peter seemed to hear the sounds of the river, and it made him think of the past. Years ago, when Peter was only 10 years old, his mother and father had fallen into the river. They were never seen again. The people in Centerville said this terrible thing happened because Peter's mother and father did not believe all the stories about the caves.

One of the stories the people of Centerville told was about Peter. They said that the first child of anyone who fell in the river and was lost would some day have to meet the One from Below.

Peter had never understood who the One from Below was. Now and then he had thought about some terrible thing that might be in the caves. Still something always made him want to return to them. At least it had when he was too young to know better.

At last—Centerville! Peter could see the lights of the town as he drove. He was getting nearer. He would soon be at the bridge, and then he would be in Centerville. In one way, he was glad to be coming back. In another way, he couldn't help but be a little sad. He thought of his mother and father as he drove over the bridge. He didn't even look down at the fast waters under the bridge. He just kept on driving. Now he was in Centerville. It was only a little way to Anne's house.

Peter didn't know why Anne had stayed in Centerville. But she always sounded happy when he spoke to her on the phone. There it is! Anne's house. He stopped the car and looked at the house. Even though it was a dark night, Peter wanted to look at it for just a minute. It was the same house he and Anne had lived in when they were children.

Suddenly Anne opened the door. "Peter! You're here—at last!"

" Peter! You're here—at last!"

CHAPTER 2

Home Again

Peter got out of the car and ran up the front steps. "Anne, you look great!"

Inside the house it was bright and warm. Even though it was late, Tom and the three kids were waiting up to see Peter.

The kids had all grown. They had been little the last time Peter saw them. Now Jasper, the oldest, was almost as tall as Peter.

"Have a seat, Peter," Tom said. "What's new?"

Before Peter could answer Tom, Jasper said, "Are you here to go back into Montauk Cave?"

"Jasper," Anne said, "wait. Your uncle just got here. Let him rest for a few minutes. Peter, can I get you some coffee?"

"You sure can, Anne," Peter said. "Jasper, I'm not here to go to the caves. I'm here to write a book *about* the caves and also to speak with

Mother Jerome about some of the stories and legends."

"Mother Jerome!" Susie said in a loud voice.

"Well, I hope I can see her," Peter said. "Maybe she won't want to see me."

"Won't you take us to the cave, Uncle Peter?" Jasper asked.

"That's up to your folks," Peter answered. "I can't stay in Centerville too long. I won't have that much time."

"Peter, I really don't want the kids going into the caves," Anne said.

Peter smiled at the three young people. "You heard what your mother said."

"Well, let me think about it," Anne said as she looked at three gloomy faces.

"Have you seen Mother Jerome?" Peter asked Tom.

"No one has, Peter, for a long time. She still lives way back up in the hills in Hazelgreen. She doesn't come into town. She stays there all alone with her old cat," Tom said. "People say she can't see any more. She just sits on her front porch all day."

Owen walked over to his uncle. "I don't want to see that old Mother Jerome, but I sure hope you can take us to the caves, Uncle Peter."

Peter smiled at him. "Let's wait and see how your mother feels about it. We'll have some good times while I'm here anyway."

"Mom," Jasper said, "I think the three of us will head off to bed. You and Dad and Uncle Peter want to talk. Anyway, it's late."

Owen and Susie groaned, but they followed their older brother upstairs.

"Good night, all of you," Peter called.

"Peter," Anne said, "maybe those caves don't scare you, but they scare me. I don't want my kids going in them."

Peter looked at Anne. "You're wrong, Sis. They scare me, too."

CHAPTER 3

The Power of the Caves

Up in the hills near Hazelgreen an old, old lady sat on her porch. She was waiting. No one had told her that Peter Cooper was back in Centerville. But she knew. Her yellow cat sat at her feet. Her white hair was pulled around her head. She just sat in her rocking chair and waited. Peter would soon be there. She knew.

Back in Centerville, the sun seemed to rise early that first Saturday morning Peter was back home. It was time to go to see Mother Jerome. It wasn't far up in the hills to Hazelgreen. But the road was old and full of holes. He wouldn't be able to drive fast.

I might as well admit it, Peter thought. I really don't want to go. But I've got to. She knows more about the stories and legends of Mokane Valley than anyone else. He got out of bed. He could hear Jasper, Owen, and Susie in the yard.

He got dressed and went downstairs for coffee with Anne and Tom.

"Good morning, Peter," Tom said, "I see you slept through all the noise this morning."

"I sure did. I was tired from that long ride into the Valley last night," Peter answered.

"Anne," Tom said, "I have to drive the pickup into town for some spare parts. I have to go now or I won't get the car fixed by Monday."

"OK," Anne said. "While you're in town, pick up some food. Here's a list of what I need. By the way, where are the kids?"

"They're in the yard," Tom said as he went out the back door.

"Well," Peter said, "I think I'd better be on my way, too. It will take me some time to get to Hazelgreen."

"What if Mother Jerome isn't there?" Anne asked.

"Oh, she'll be there," Peter said. "Where would she go?"

"Well, try to get home for lunch," Anne smiled. "and we'll talk about the good old days."

Anne and Peter said goodbye. Anne began to clear the dishes off the table, and Peter drove away in his car.

Out in the yard, away from the house, Jasper,

Outside in the yard, Jasper, Owen, and Susie were talking about the cave.

Owen, and Susie were talking about the caves. They had all wanted to go into them for a long time. Before Peter had come, they were sure they could talk him into taking them. But now it didn't look good. Their mother didn't want them to go, and Uncle Peter didn't seem to want to go much either. They heard their uncle leave.

"Let's go by ourselves," Jasper said. "I know how to get there."

"Let's! But we'll need some things, won't we?" Susie asked.

"Yeah," Owen said. "We'll need three flashlights, for sure."

"And how about some food, too?" Susie said.

"What will we need food for?" Jasper asked.

"Oh, we might want to stop and eat along the way," Susie answered.

Owen went into the house and got three flashlights. Susie made sure her mother had left the kitchen and then got some bread and apples and cheese. Just to be safe, Jasper took some candles, matches, and rope.

In a few minutes they all met outside near the back gate. They were almost ready to leave when Jasper said, "Wait a minute. I think we should have some water, too." He ran back inside the house, got his canteen, and filled it.

Montauk Cave was the biggest cave in the Valley. Jasper, Owen, and Susie had heard many of the legends. They heard the one about people who went in and never came out. And the one about monsters. And the stories about strange animals who lived in the caves. In the daytime the stories didn't seem real. At night, sitting around a camp fire, they seemed very real.

Jasper, Owen, and Susie started off. Their path led them through the hills. Jasper knew the way so he acted as the leader.

"I wonder if we should have told Mom where we were going," Owen said.

"Oh, don't worry. We'll be back in time for dinner," Jasper said.

"Susie," Owen said, "are you getting scared?"

Yes, Susie was getting scared. At first she had wanted to go. Now she wasn't so sure about all of this. Even Owen was less and less sure as they got nearer to the cave.

Jasper could see that his sister and brother were not feeling so brave now. He had to say something to make them feel better. Maybe he should not have taken them along, he thought. But too late for that now.

"Look," he said, "We're doing this to help Uncle Peter. He needs to know if Montauk Cave is still the same as it was when he was a kid. There's nothing to worry about. We'll all stay together inside the cave. We each have a flashlight, and I have candles. I also brought some chalk. We can mark the walls of the caves as we walk through them. That way we can't get lost. So there's nothing to worry about."

Owen and Susie began to feel a bit better.

Susie said, "Well, Owen and I don't want to go in very far, Jasper. When we get tired, we can sit down and wait for you to come back."

"Don't worry," Jasper said. "We won't go into the cave very far. Just far enough to see some neat things."

They had been walking for about an hour when Jasper saw the hill with the opening to the caves. "There it is," he called out.

The three walked up the hill to the opening. Lots of trees and bushes grew around the opening. But Jasper knew how to get to it. They all were feeling a little scared—but excited!

Jasper went in first. The opening was small, and it was very dark inside. But he wanted to show Owen and Susie it was safe. "Come on in," he yelled. His voice seemed very far away.

Owen and Susie followed Jasper into the cave. They had to bend down to get through the opening. It was not only dark but very, very cold. They turned on their flashlights and saw Jasper. He turned his flashlight on, too.

"Now listen," he said, "stay close to each other. Say something every once in a while. Then we'll know that everyone is here. Keep your flashlights on. If I go too fast, let me know. OK?"

They started off. They seemed to be walking in a long, long hall that was not very wide. The hall seemed to go down hill. They could reach out and touch the wet, cold walls. All they could see ahead was darkness. Not a bit of light—except for their flashlights.

Jasper stopped. He took the chalk out of his pocket and made a big X on the wall.

"Why did you do that?" Owen asked.

"So we'll know this is the way out. I'll make a mark like that every time we stop. Then when we come back this way, we can look for the marks," Jasper answered.

Susie was flashing her light all around the long hall.

"That's a good idea," Jasper said. "Look for things that you won't forget. It's like being outside. You won't forget what some rocks look like."

"Look at that one," Susie called. "It looks like a skull!"

"Boo!" Owen yelled.

Susie jumped. Then she started to laugh.

"OK, we'll have to start moving again before we get too cold," Jasper said. And then he called out in a loud voice, "Off we go."

The three of them heard coming back at them, "...go...go...go...go-o-o-o."

Susie grabbed Owen's arm, but Jasper said, "Don't worry. It's just an echo. It won't hurt you. Come on."

"Boy," said Owen, "this place is spooky. We should come here for Halloween."

"Not me," Susie said. "Once will be plenty for me."

"Aw, come on," Jasper smiled. "This is going to be fun. And think how much we'll have to tell Uncle Peter."

CHAPTER 4

Mother Jerome's Warning

Peter reached Mother Jerome's house high in the hills. He stopped his car. But before he could get out, a yellow cat ran in front of him. A yellow cat! He sat in the car for a minute. Did Mother Jerome make that happen? He shook his head. What a foolish thought!

Mother Jerome was standing on the front porch of her old house. She was waiting for him. She seemed to know he was coming.

"So, Peter, you're back," was all she said. "Come up here and talk to me."

Peter looked at her. Could she see? She was very old. But she looked the very same as she had looked years ago when he was a little boy.

He walked up the stairs. She put out her hand for Peter. He shook it. It was cold and strong like a piece of steel.

"Did you make that yellow cat run out in front of me?" Peter asked.

"A yellow cat is good luck, Peter," Mother Jerome said. "Did you forget that after you left us? I think you have forgotten many things."

Peter thought about the times when he was little. He would feel brave and go to visit Mother Jerome. She told him all kinds of stories about the Valley and the caves. And here he was. A man. But back at Mother Jerome's.

"Come sit with me, Peter. Why did you *really* come back to Mokane Valley? You told me you would never come back," she said.

"I have a new job, Mother Jerome," Peter answered.

"Yes, I know all about it," said Mother Jerome as she slowly rocked.

How did she know, Peter thought. How *could* she know?

"Yes, you believe you are here to write about the stories and legends of Mokane Valley. Isn't that right?" she said.

Mother Jerome was just the same. She always knew things even though no one told them to her. She just seemed to know. That is why she made Peter feel creepy.

"You know more about the stories and legends of the Valley than anyone else. That's why I've come to see you. Will you help me?" he asked.

"You know I will, don't you, Peter?" she said. "But first have a cup of my tea." She got up and brought Peter a cup of green tea. He took a sip.

"It's good," he said.

"It should be," she answered. "I made it myself from some weeds that grow up on the hill."

Peter drank only a little of the tea. He wasn't sure what she had made it from.

"Go on, have some more," she said.

"Oh, that's fine," he said. "Mother Jerome, I must . . ."

"Yes, you must talk to me and leave. You must go back with all the stories. You must . . . You must . . . You must," she said.

Peter looked at her. She looked back at him with her green eyes. No, she looked *through* him with those eyes.

"Peter, there are things you have to know now that you are back. You think you came here because of the book you are going to write, don't you? Oh, no, you didn't, Peter. You *had* to come back. You were *called* back to the Valley."

Then she stopped rocking. "The One from Below is waiting for you, Peter."

Peter felt cold, then hot, then cold again. He thought about when he was a little boy. He had heard about the One from Below. It had scared him then, and it scared him now.

He jumped up. "No! No! I don't even know what you are talking about!"

"Sit down, Peter," she said. "Let me tell you about the legends. Let me tell you about the things we know nothing about." She started to rock in her chair.

Peter felt himself grow weak. Was it the rock, rock, rock of her chair? Or the tea? Or her green eyes looking through him? He wanted to run down the steps of the porch and leave. But he couldn't. He just sat there.

"These things, Peter," she went on, "are everywhere. We can't see them. We can't hear them. But they're with us. Sometimes right with us. You call our legend a silly thing, don't you? No, Peter, it is not silly. You will know very soon." Then she picked up her yellow cat.

"You didn't like the yellow cat running in front of your car, did you?" she asked. "But how do you know that this cat is an animal? How do you know that, Peter? And how do you know a dream isn't real? You don't know that, Peter. Dreams can be real."

Peter listened. Again it was quiet. And again he felt her green eyes looking right into him. He couldn't say anything. He just listened.

"You have made fun of us here in the Valley,

Peter. We think that when a dog barks at the moon, someone will die. But you laugh at that. My poor Peter. You have so much to learn and so little time to learn it," she said.

He looked at her. He knew she was trying to tell him something. But he didn't know what it was. "What do you mean?" he asked very quietly.

"I mean this. There are many worlds. You know only this one you are in. You were chosen to go to one of the other worlds. You, Peter, have been chosen to meet the One from Below."

Peter didn't want to hear another word. He tried to get up from his chair, but he could not.

"The Mokane Valley is rich," Mother Jerome said. She pointed to the hills around Hazelgreen. "The Mokane Valley was chosen, too, a long, long, long time ago. It is home not only to us, but to *them*. Our legends and stories are good luck for us. They keep us safe from the world below. Only those who do not believe have something to fear."

"Mother Jerome," Peter said, "I don't understand. You're talking about things I don't believe in. And you say they are real."

"Peter, Peter," she said. "You don't remember. You believed in them when you lived here. But after you left, you came to believe they were silly."

She was right. Peter had believed in all these things when he was little. People who grew up in the Valley and who stayed there still believed them. But he had left.

"In Montauk Cave. That's where you will find it," she said. "It has no eyes, but it sees all that happens here in our Valley. If you do not go to it, Peter, I tell you that someone will die. Die! And it will be your fault, Peter. All your fault!"

"If you do not go to it, someone will die."

said, "when will we ever be able
gain? Come on. Just five more
e'll leave."
their snack and started over to
back of it was yet another big
one was different. As soon as
Jasper knew something was

avern started to move up and
kind of noise started. Jasper,
couldn't move. They held onto
d they gone too far into the

We'll never get out of here!"
sper said.
shed Susie down. "What was
"Who pushed me?"
bats in here. Lots of them,"
was right. Bats were flying all
Thousands of them, and their
three feet across. They didn't
s. They were making an awful
everywhere. They flew down at
d Susie. One made a deep cut

rms. Shine your flashlights on
ld scare them," Jasper yelled.
here!"

CHAPTER 5

Terror in the Montauk

They had never seen anything like Montauk. Jasper, Owen, and Susie walked on and on through it. Sometimes they had to crawl. But they kept on going. They forgot what time it was.

Up to this time, they had not seen anything except walls. Now they were deep enough in the cave to see other things.

Susie suddenly yelled, "Stop! Jasper and Owen, look at this." She had her flashlight on the wall. Something white with long feelers and no eyes was sitting on a rock. "What is it?"

"It's a cricket," Jasper said. "It has no eyes because it doesn't need them here in the caves where there is no light. It is born here, and it dies here. It moves by using its feelers."

"Do you think we'll see more animals like that?" Owen asked.

"Well, we might. They say there is a big, big

room deep in the cave. It has a pool. There are fish that live in the pool. And they don't need eyes either," Jasper said.

At first all they had heard as they had moved through the cave was their own voices. Now they started to hear other things.

"I think I can hear the sound of water," Owen said.

"You probably do," said Jasper. "We might be under the Mokane River. Or we could be near the big room."

"A big room? Down here?" Susie asked.

"Well, it's not a room like you think, Susie," Jasper answered. "It's a place down here that is so big, people call it the main cavern of the cave."

As they kept on walking, the hallway got smaller and smaller. Soon they had to crawl again. Then Jasper's flashlight showed a small hole. They could feel air coming from it.

"Oh, the air coming through that hole feels cold," Owen said.

"That small hole will take us to the main cavern of the cave," Jasper said.

"But it's so small," Susie said. "We can't get through it."

"Oh, yes, we can. I'll show you how," Jasper

said. "Y
arm, the
you. Lik
through
other sid
then Ow
Susie
all stood
that the
ants. Wa
many ye
creepy. T
Near the
where th
cold in t
"Let's
up."
They s
cheese,
bread in
to get it.
"See,"
the bread
Susie
want to
said.
"All ri
one more

"Yeah," Owen
to get back here
minutes. Then w
They finished
another wall. In
cavern, but this
they were in it,
wrong!
Suddenly the
down. A terrible
Owen, and Susie
one another. Ha
caves?
Owen yelled, "
"Shut up!" Ja
Something pu
that?" she yelled.
"There are big
Jasper yelled. He
over the cavern.
wings were abou
like the flashligh
noise and flying
Jasper, Owen, a
on Owen's arm.
"Wave your a
them. That shou
"Let's get out of

One made a deep cut on Owen's arm.

They turned around to get back to the other side of the wall. Suddenly Owen smelled something terrible. The three of them stopped in their tracks. They couldn't move.

"It's coming from there," Jasper yelled. In a small hole in the cavern something was happening. It was like death coming to life!

CHAPTER 6

Missing!

After his visit with Mother Jerome, Peter's world was no longer the same. His mind felt empty as he drove back to his sister's home. His eyes saw nothing in the green valley below. Peter now knew more than any man should know.

Anne was out front when he arrived. "Peter! Peter!" she shouted from the porch. "Have you seen the kids? They're not home."

Peter got out of the car and walked to his sister. He didn't say anything. He just walked past her into the house. She came after him.

"Peter, I don't know where they've gone. It's almost four o'clock. I haven't seen the kids since you left this morning." Anne was scared. She knew something was wrong. "I looked for the flashlights. All of them were gone. Peter! Peter! Listen to me!"

Peter was quiet. He looked at Anne. He didn't say anything.

Then she knew, too. "You know, don't you? They're in the cave, aren't they?" she yelled.

Peter knew. He hadn't seen or heard them, but he knew they were in the cave. Just like he knew he would have to go inside the Montauk himself.

"Yes," he said, "they're in the cave. Get into the car. We must try to get them out before it's too late."

Anne and Peter ran to the car. They drove over the bumpy roads as fast as they could. It seemed they would never get there. They didn't say a word to one another. Both of them knew something was wrong. As soon as Peter stopped the car, they both jumped out and ran to the opening of the Montauk. Peter wished he could turn around and run away. But it was no use. This day had been planned for him long, long ago.

"Oh, Peter, why did they do it? Why did they go in there?" Anne cried.

Peter heard his sister's words. Jasper, Owen, and Susie were in danger. He knew it. He felt fear.

At first, Anne didn't seem to smell it, but Peter did. That terrible smell from deep inside the cave was now coming out of the opening near where they were standing. It seemed to move around them as if it were alive. Then they heard voices. Jasper and then Susie came running out of the cave into the sunlight.

"Oh, Mom," Susie said, "it was terrible. There were thousands of big bats in there. They were all over us!"

Jasper and then Susie came running out of the cave into the sunlight.

"Where's Owen?" Anne yelled.

"He was right in back of us," Jasper said. "I heard him. I saw his flashlight. We marked our way with chalk. That's how we got out so fast."

Peter grabbed his arm. "Where did you go, Jasper? And why?"

"We were in the main cavern, Uncle Peter," Jasper said. "The bats came over us all of a sudden. And then when that terrible smell came into the cave, we started to run. I'm really sorry. We wanted to help you with your book."

"I must go in there," Peter said. "I must go in alone. Everyone wait right here. Don't anyone come with me." He grabbed Jasper's flashlight.

Peter bent low and walked into the cave—and into the darkness of Montauk.

CHAPTER 7

The Chosen

Peter walked into the cave alone. He had Jasper's flashlight. But, even so, the cave before him seemed as if it went on and on and would never stop. This dark hole was cold as winter. It seemed to be saying, "Come, Peter. Come." It seemed to be calling him to a place he never wanted to go.

He started to walk fast. Sometimes he had to bend down. Sometimes he had to crawl. Sometimes he had to go through small holes. The flashlight on the walls showed where Jasper had made marks with the chalk. But those marks didn't seem to matter to him. He was moving as fast as he could. He was rushing to meet what waited ahead.

Owen sat on the floor of the cave. He knew Jasper and Susie must be out of the cave by this time. His arm hurt where the bat had hit him. He had lost his flashlight. It had dropped out of his hands and rolled down and down. Then he couldn't see it any more. He tried to get the candle Jasper had given him out of his pocket. He found one—but Jasper had the matches!

"Owen! Owen! It's Uncle Peter. Can you hear me?" Peter called. In the long, dark halls of the Cave, Owen couldn't hear Peter. Sometimes he thought he heard ". . . hear me . . . hear me . . . hear me . . . hear me" but that was all.

Even Peter didn't hear his own words as he called out. All he could hear were the words of Mother Jerome. What she had said was still in his mind. He heard those words over and over again. "Someone will die . . . It will be your fault . . . Someone will die . . . It will be your fault . . . You must go to the cave . . ."

Peter kept on running and calling for Owen. And in his mind was: Why? Why? Why have I been chosen? Why? Why?

Suddenly a hand came out of the darkness. It pulled at Peter. He turned around to hit hard at whatever was there.

It was Owen. He was sitting on the floor. Cold as ice!

"Owen! At last! Are you OK?" Peter reached out to help Owen get up.

"I've been so scared! I was here alone in the dark with this cat," Owen said.

With a cat!

Peter looked down at Owen. There on his lap was Mother Jerome's yellow cat! "Where did you find that cat?" Peter asked.

"I was sitting here. I didn't know what to do. Then the cat came and sat on my lap. I felt better then," Owen said.

Peter couldn't believe what he was seeing. How did the cat get into the cave? What was it doing so far from home? How did it find Owen? Why was it just sitting there looking up at Peter with its green eyes?

Green eyes? Green eyes? Mother Jerome's green eyes!

Was this the warning Mother Jerome had given him? "Someone will die . . . It will be your fault . . . Someone will die . . .Unless you go to the cave, it will be your fault . . ." Was Owen the one he had to save?

"Where are Jasper and Susie?" Owen asked.

"They're OK. But what about you?" Peter asked.

"My flashlight rolled away from me. I was trying to light my candle. But I couldn't. I didn't have any matches. But then I thought, what if I did light my candle and it went out? Don't you know, Uncle Peter? If a candle burns out by itself, someone will die. I was scared to light it—even if I could. But I felt better after the cat came," Owen said.

"No! No! Nothing is going to hurt you—or anyone," Peter said. "Everything is OK. Just get out of here as fast as you can. Here, take my

"Don't you know, Uncle Peter? If a candle burns out by itself, someone will die."

flashlight and go. Follow the marks Jasper put on the walls. You'll be safe, Owen, if you don't look back. Just keep moving and don't look back."

Peter pushed Owen to get him started. He kept on calling out, "Keep moving, Owen. Don't look back. You're OK. It isn't far."

Now Peter was alone. He looked around. The cat was gone. He took the candle Owen had left and lighted it. He moved on with just the candle to light his way. He finally reached the hole that went into the main cavern of the Montauk. The smell was terrible. It was so bad, he felt sick. It seemed to rush to him, to be all around him. When he got through the hole and was inside the cavern, he could see something moving on the floor. No! There were *many* things moving around.

Snakes! Thousands of them. All sizes. They crawled all over each other. They were everywhere. Where did they come from? He moved back against the wall and felt hundreds of bugs trying to crawl on him. He tried to brush them off. Then the bats started to come after him. There were thousands of them flying around the cavern. Only the light from his candle kept them away. He stopped for a minute. He was breathing hard.

And then—oh, no!—something started to rise out of the water in the main cavern. Steam came out of the water. The floor where he stood started to shake.

Peter yelled. The thing that grew in front of him kept growing and growing. Finally, it grew so big, it brushed away the bats from the top of the cavern. It was huge, and that terrible smell was all around it.

Peter found a small place to crawl into. He yelled, "Help me! Help me!" But no one could. No one answered his calls.

Huge spiders, as big as his hands, started to drop on him. They had found his hiding place. They were crawling all over him.

Peter was living a nightmare. This was like a terrible dream—but it wasn't a dream. The room started to spin around. The years passed. Peter thought he saw his parents. In the nightmare the cavern spun again. He saw Anne and Susie waiting for him outside. He saw Jasper standing by the opening of the cave. He saw Owen running out of the cave to safety. Then he saw Mother Jerome. She was sitting on her porch at Hazelgreen with her yellow cat.

Was all of this real? He pulled at his hair, but it didn't hurt. His heart was pounding. Alone in the cavern, he was sure his nightmare would never end.

The thing that had come out of the water—the thing that smelled so terrible—moved in front of him. It moved all around. It seemed to grow stronger as Peter cried out to be saved. He looked as it moved closer and closer to him. As its darkness began to choke him, Peter said, "Yes! Yes! Yes! I believe!"

Could it be true? With the words "I believe," the terrible thing moved away from him.

And then Peter got up and started to run through the darkness of Montauk Cave. As he ran, he felt that the cave was trying to pull him back in. Somehow, some way, he kept running through the darkness. Never did he look back. He had played in the cave so many times as a child he knew the way out well. But never had it seemed so far!

Now, as he ran, all the legends of the Mokane Valley seemed to call out to him. He listened to them and said them over and over to himself. He believed! He was not scared any more. He believed! Now he felt safe. Finally, he reached the cave opening—and fell on the ground.

Anne helped Peter to the car. He could not see. He had been blinded by the evil of Montauk

Cave. It would be many weeks before he would be able to see again. And his sight would always be dim.

That night Mother Jerome sat alone on her porch. Her yellow cat was on her lap. "Yes, Peter, it is all true. And now, at last, you believe," she said to herself softly.

"And now, at last, you believe."

CHAPTER 8

Hazelgreen

Peter sat on the porch of Mother Jerome's house. He was sitting in Mother Jerome's chair. A white cat with green eyes sat in his lap.

How long had he been here? Days? Weeks? Months? Years? He didn't know, and it didn't matter. Anne and Tom came to see him once in a while. But not the kids.

After that terrible day in the cave, Peter knew he could never leave the Valley again. And then, suddenly, Mother Jerome had died. Then it was all very clear. Now that she was gone, he must be the one to guard the legends of the Valley.

Now he just sat all day long. Sometimes people from Centerville would come to ask Uncle Peter to tell them about the stories and legends of Mokane Valley. And he would tell them all they wanted to know.

Peter now had white hair. That day – that terrible day in the cave—his hair had turned white. He looked old—like Mother Jerome—and he knew all the legends as well as she had known them.

Suddenly he stopped rocking and listened. He heard a car coming up the hill to the house. The cat jumped out of his lap and ran down the front steps.

A pretty young woman got out of the car. "I hope I didn't hit your cat. It ran right in front of my car," she said.

"No, she's all right," he answered. The cat ran back up on the porch and jumped into Peter's lap.

"You're Uncle Peter, aren't you?" the young woman asked.

"Yes, you are at the right place," he answered.

The young lady walked up the stairs and sat down.

"My name is Ellie Hopper. I'm from Kelso about 100 miles from here," she said.

"Yes," Peter said, "I knew you were coming to see me."

Ellie Hopper just looked at Peter. She looked into his green eyes. He was looking right at her, but he seemed to be looking *through* her.

"You work for an oil company, and you are

Suddenly he stopped rocking and listened. He heard a car coming up the hill to the house. The cat jumped out of his lap and ran down the front steps.

here to find out if there is oil in the Mokane Valley. Isn't that right?" he asked.

"Yes, that is right," she answered. She couldn't figure out how Uncle Peter could have known that. But, she thought, all the people in the

Valley know one another. Maybe word had gotten to Uncle Peter that she was coming.

"Before we talk," said Peter, "have a cup of my tea." He got up and brought Ellie a cup of green tea. She took a sip.

"It's good," she said.

"It should be," he answered. "I made it myself from some weeds that grow up on the hill."

Ellie drank only a little of the tea. She wasn't sure what he had made it from.

"Go on, have some more," he said.

"Oh, that's fine," she said. "Uncle Peter, people tell me that you know more about the Valley than anyone else. So I want to ask if you will . . ." She stopped.

"Yes," said Uncle Peter, "you want to know if I will tell you where the oil is."

"That's right," she said.

"Oh, yes," he said. "There is oil here in the Valley. Lots of it.'

"You know, Uncle Peter," she said, "I was born here in the Valley, but when I was a little girl, my parents died, and I went to live with my aunt in Kelso."

"Yes, your Aunt Louise," he said. "A nice lady, but she didn't believe in the legends of our Valley," Peter said.

"Well, no, she didn't. Neither did my parents. And I don't either," said Ellie.

"Oh, you will. You must. You see, there is oil here. Lots of it. But it is all in the Montauk Cave. You must go there to find it. You see, Ellie, you have been chosen."